To Evie and Ted

The Adventures of
Willowbe Woods

Melissa

The Fairy Princess

with love

Maisy Day

The Adventures of
Willowbe Woods

Melissa

The Fairy Princess

Maisy Day

Cover illustration by Flora Daneman

ISBN: 9798567908013

PublishNation
www.publishnation.co.uk

For Olivia and Edward

Acknowledgements

If I think back to when I first started my Willowbe Woods adventures I need to trace my steps back all the way to my childhood. I grew up in rural Pembrokeshire in South West Wales and as the daughter of hard working farmers, my younger years were spent as much working as playing. Days were long and times were not always easy but we lived surrounded by the most magical woods and beautiful countryside. Places that became a natural playground for my sisters and I to explore and indulge our imagination in as we explored the endless paths filled with nature and wildlife. A place of adventure where no two days were ever the same. For this, the woods of Trearched Farm will always hold a special place in my heart and have inspired me to turn my imagination to writing. And when it came to writing this book, I have a few more people to thank than my childhood memories.

Thank you to my grandchildren Olivia and Edward for listening to and enjoying Gran's made-up bedtime stories. You helped me in creating tales of adventures and turning ideas into stories, which usually started because I didn't have my glasses and so had to think on the spot!

Thank you to my two daughters. To Sarah, for all your help with editing and the writing process and to Katherine for all your creative input and ideas.

A big thank you also to my husband Tom for his ongoing support in my dream to write a book.

And finally thank you to the incredibly talented Flora Daneman who has beautifully captured the essence of all the characters in this book with her wonderful cover illustration.

The Adventures of
Willowbe Woods

Melissa

The Fairy Princess

Chapter 1

Once upon a time there was a little girl called Olivia who lived in a beautiful rose clad cottage at the edge of Willowbe woods with her mummy, daddy and her little brother Edward. Each day Olivia would go to play in the woods. The woods held a very special secret that only Olivia knew. Underneath the old oak tree, deep in its old twisted roots, lived Melissa the fairy princess.

Melissa would wave her magic wand and sprinkle fairy dust on Olivia's head. Abracadabra! Olivia would be transformed into a beautiful fairy with silvery wings and a sparkly dress that shimmered in the rays of sunlight that shone through the branches of the old oak tree.

They would spend the day skipping and playing with Melissa's friends. There was Harry the hedgehog with his prickly back and soft cuddly tummy, Winnie the mouse with her wispy tickly long tail, Freddie the frog with his lanky long legs, the very naughty Ronnie the rabbit, Sammy the squirrel and Oscar the wise old owl who watched over them all.

Chapter 2

Meanwhile back at the cottage, Edward was getting rather tired of being left behind to play by himself whilst Olivia slipped away deep into the woods. He had asked Olivia if he could go with her today, but Olivia had replied, "you are my little brother Edward and you are not allowed to come with me." So he decided to go on his very own adventure. He always kept his rucksack packed under his bed, ready for this very sort of occasion. The only thing left to pack was the one item that was most important to Edward. His picnic. When his mummy wasn't looking, Edward sneaked into the kitchen and quietly made a sandwich and grabbed an apple, biscuit and drink. He waited until Olivia had disappeared out of sight and then grabbed his rucksack and set out of the cottage towards the woods on his first real adventure. Even the storm from the night before, which had left the day grey and damp, was not going to put him off going. As he walked deeper into the woods, he didn't want to admit it, but he started to feel a little scared. He had never been this far from home on his own before. He took a deep breath and said to himself, "come on Edward, you're not scared. This is an adventure and adventures are fun." He continued walking along the path through the tall and rustling trees when he realised he was already starting to feel a little hungry - Edward was always hungry! He came across a tree stump and thought, "what a great spot to eat my picnic."

As he sat eating his lunch, a squirrel came and sat beside him. "Hi Edward", said Sammy. Edward could not believe his ears. Had the squirrel just spoken to him, and how did he know his name? Could he really talk to the animals and the animals talk to him? "This is so exciting and so much fun," he said to himself. "No wonder Olivia loves coming here so much. This is such a magical place. What an adventure I am going to have."

Edward sat and chatted to Sammy who wondered what he was doing in the woods on his own. He told Sammy all about how his big sister Olivia was always coming to the woods and said what fun she had so he thought he would go on his own adventure and see the woods for himself. As Sammy and Edward sat on the tree trunk together, Edward's fears about being far away from home were soon long gone. That was, until all of a sudden, a cold white mist descended over the woods. Edward suddenly felt cold and wanted to go but when he got up, he could no longer see which path he had taken and which way led to home. Edward started to sob. "Don't worry," said Sammy, "I will guide you through the woods. We will find my friends and we can have an adventure together."

Chapter 3

The storm had raged and rumbled all night and had left the morning colder and darker than usual, but this did not put Olivia off from going out. She headed for the woods, as she often did, to find Melissa. When she got there she couldn't find her anywhere. She was not in her usual place underneath the knotted roots of the oak tree. All of a sudden Olivia had a feeling that all was not well. It was too quiet. None of her friends were anywhere to be seen.

Whatever was the matter? Could it have something to do with the storm from last night? The sky was still grey and rumbly and all did not feel right. Was it the naughty elves and pixies who had a tendency to play jokes on Melissa and her friends? Had they been up to their old tricks and mischief again?

Suddenly something caught Olivia's eye amongst the leaves surrounding the roots of the tree. It was Melissa's magic wand. "Oh no," whispered Olivia to herself in panic. "Melissa does not go anywhere without her magic wand. Whatever can the matter be."

At that moment a swishing noise came from above. Oscar the wise old owl swooped down. "Good morning Olivia," he hooted. When Olivia did not answer he realised something was amiss and asked, "whatever is the matter dear child?"

"Oh dear Oscar," Olivia sobbed, "I can't find Melissa and she has dropped her magic wand. Without her magic wand her wings do not work. Where is everybody else?" she asked. "I don't know," Oscar replied.

All of a sudden, adding to the gloom and feeling that something was wrong, a cold white mist descended on them. Oscar said he would fly around and see if he could find where they all might be.

As the mist continued to blanket the woods, a faint and high pitched noise, similar to that of tiny flutes, could be heard in the distance. Unbeknown to Olivia, Edward and the animals of the woods, it was the pixies and elves dancing for joy with the mischief they were causing.

As Oscar swooped away, Olivia sat all alone on the roots and continued to sob. Freddie the frog, tucked under a nearby stone, heard Olivia crying and came leaping across to find out what the matter was.

"Where is everybody Freddie?" Olivia asked, happy to see another friendly face. "I am not sure Olivia. We were all sitting under the tree roots last night when there was loud crash and everybody disappeared. I have only seen Sammy the squirrel. He is having an adventure with a new friend he helped when the mist came down."

"Oscar is flying around as we speak to see if he can see where everyone might be," said Olivia.

"Do not be so sad Olivia. Come on! Let's go together and see if we can find Melissa and the others," said Freddie . So with a leap and a jump, Freddie and Olivia set off to continue the search.

"You are so kind Freddie, thank you for helping me."

Chapter 4

The pixies and elves watched on as Olivia, Freddie, Edward and Sammy struggled through the woods. It was difficult to see where they were going.

Fed up of not being allowed to join in and play with Melissa and the other animals, they had cast a spell which covered the whole of the woods in the thick white mist. Peaking out from their well hidden nooks and crannies, they were feeling rather amused with themselves until they saw how sad Olivia was and that, whilst he wouldn't admit it, Edward was acting a little braver than he actually felt. They started to realise that perhaps the spell they had cast was not going to make them very popular and that what they had done was not very kind. Maybe not everyone liked them playing tricks and causing mischief all the time.

Meanwhile Edward and Sammy were having fun exploring the woods, climbing trees and looking for acorns, totally unaware that things were amiss elsewhere. Even though the mist made it difficult to see, with Sammy's help he was guided through the woods. He was having so much fun.

Chapter 5

Despite the mist, Freddie and Olivia continued through the woods until they stumbled upon Harry the hedgehog. "Have you seen Melissa?" Asked Olivia. "No," said Harry as he stretched out is prickly back, "I haven't seen anybody." "But where is everybody?" screeched Olivia, so loud it made Harry and Freddie jump. They suddenly both realised how frightened and upset Olivia really was.

Harry explained. "Last night there was a loud bang, the storm was raging and the wind and rain lashed against the oak tree. All of a sudden there was a loud bang frightening us all and causing everyone to scatter. When we woke up this morning it was so strange. We could not see the sunrise as the skies were still grey and dull then a strange white mist descended on us all." Harry, still feeling a little nervous and not wanting to be by himself, asked if he could join in the search. "It would be better if we could all be together," said Harry.

Not too far away, Ronnie the rabbit, who had a tendency to be a liitle naughty, emerged from his den. He stretched out his legs before doing a couple of hops. "Gosh it's very quiet," he said to himself, "why has no-one come to play today? And what is this strange mist?" He pricked up his ears. In the distance he could hear the sound of voices and they seemed to be creeping closer. He looked out into the mist and as the voices became clearer, out emerged Olivia, Freddie and Harry coming along the path. "Oh thank goodness Ronnie," Olivia said. "Have you seen Melissa? She is missing and I found her wand amongst the leaves under the old oak tree. Without her wand she cannot do her magic."

"I wondered where everybody was," said Ronnie. "I will join you and we can look for her together."

Just then, Winnie the mouse appeared from under her pile of leaves where she lived. "Oh thank goodness. I am so happy to see you all. I have been so scared. I could not find anybody and when I saw the mist coming, I crept back under my pile of leaves."

"Winnie!" Said Olivia, equally as happy to see her. "Melissa is missing."

"Oh no!" Winnie whimpered. "Shall we all stay together and see if we can find her?" And with a flick of her long wispy tail, Winnie joined in the search.

Chapter 6

All of this adventuring and talking to animals was making Edward hungry. "Can we stop and have a snack?" Edward asked his new friend. Sammy sat beside Edward and tucked into an acorn he found next to a leaf as Edward started on his apple. "Look Sammy!" Edward said. "Look at those beautiful toadstools, they are magical." Just then, Edward heard a faint whimpering sound coming from underneath the toadstool. "Did you hear that Sammy? I can hear crying coming from the toadstool." Sammy and Edward cautiously tiptoed towards the vibrant red and white toadstool and to

Edward's surprise, underneath the toadstool, there was a fairy. "I don't believe it!" Edward gasped excitedly to Sammy. "Come and look. I've found a fairy!" Melissa shrieked as Edward looked over her but then she saw he was with Sammy. "Melissa, whatever are you doing hiding under the toadstool?" Sammy asked. "Oh Sammy. The naughty pixies and elves said I had to be punished for not letting them play with Olivia and all our friends."

"Olivia? Did you say Olivia?" Edward asked astonished, "my big sister Olivia?" "Yes!" said Melissa." She comes to play with me every day. She is my best friend. I sprinkle magic dust with my wand and this transforms her into a fairy just like me."

"But where is Olivia now?" Edward asked suddenly feel a little worried again. "She left for the woods this morning."

"I don't know Edward," Melissa said before starting to explain what happened the night before. "Late into the evening, as the storm was raging, there was a sudden loud bang. I was so frightened and, as I ran off, I dropped my magic wand. I was too scared to go back and look for it, so I just kept going hoping I would find my friends but then this white mist came down and I couldn't see where to go. I didn't know what else to do and I was so cold so I hid under this toadstool. Oh what will I do? Without my magic wand I have no powers. I can't do magic, I can't grant wishes, I cannot turn Olivia into a fairy and worst of all, I cannot fly."

"This mist is very strange," said Sammy thoughtfully as Edward turned to Melissa and said, "come and sit by me and get warm. I'm sure you are hungry as well. You can share my picnic with me and Sammy."

"But what about Olivia?" Melissa asked. "She will be very worried about me." "Let's finish our picnic first and then we will go together and look for the others," suggested Edward, still a little bit hungry having not yet finished his apple. "But Edward, without my magic wand I cannot fly. How will I keep up with you and Sammy, I am so small." "No problem Melissa, you can sit in my rucksack and we will go and find everybody together," Edward answered proudly.

Chapter 7

Olivia, Freddie, Harry and Winnie carried along the path. As they did Olivia thought quietly to herself, "this mist is very strange. It feels like it is made to just hang over us. As if we are being punished."

Meanwhile Oscar was flying above the trees when he suddenly caught sight of the pixies and elves giggling and chatting down below. Oscar swopped down with a swish and a glide and perched himself on the knotted roots. He stood up straight and puffed out his chest.

"Good afternoon elves and pixies and what might you all be up to on this gloomy day?" "Oh we have been having a great day Oscar. We have put a spell on the woods," they said with a mischievous chuckle. "It's to punish Melissa and all her friends for not including us in their games." Oscar drew in a deep breath and put his wing to his beak. He thought for a while then all of a sudden stood to attention.

"Elves and pixies gather round and listen to me." Owl said with his very stern voice. "The trouble with you pixies and elves is that you are always playing tricks and causing mischief. You frighten those living around you and your jokes are not very kind. You are always pinching Sammy's acorns, filling in Ronnie's home, pulling Winne's tail, taking Freddie's water, pulling Melissa's wings and playing tricks on Olivia. None of these acts are what friends do to each other. If you want the others to include you, I would start by being kinder. Then they would then let you join in with their games." The elves and pixies formed a circle and chatted to each other. On reflection they agreed that perhaps on this occasion they had gone a step too far. They hadn't really meant to make everyone so frightened and upset. "Now," Oscar said, "how about making your first act of kindness be lifting the spell you have put on the woods."

Chapter 8

Olivia held tightly onto Melissa's wand as they all walked along the path. Suddenly the mist lifted clearing the way for the sun to shine through. The woods felt safe again. Olivia could hear voices, and to her surprise coming down the path in front of them, was, could it really be, her little brother Edward and Sammy. "Olivia!" Sammy shouted. "Look who Edward has got in his rucksack."

Edward carefully lifted Melissa out of his rucksack and placed her in Olivia's hand. Melissa screamed with delight at seeing Olivia and all her friends. Suddenly something caught her eye, gleaming in Olivia's hand. She could not believe her eyes. Her magic wand! "Oh Olivia you found my magic wand I am so happy, thank you thank you," she said gratefully. Olivia handed her the wand and Melissa's face shone with delight. "I can use my magic wand to magic us all back to the oak tree. Come on everybody!" With a swish and a flick, Melissa waved her magic wand and they all flew into the air back to the oak tree. Edward screamed with delight. "We can fly!"

When they arrived, they were all surprised to see Oscar talking to the pixies and elves. "I am so pleased to see that you are all safe and sound," said Oscar. "Gather round everybody," he said firmly and then went on to tell them all about what the pixies and elves had been up to. How they had cast the spell on the woods which caused the mist. "Now," he said turning towards the pixies and elves who were all a little pink faced. "The pixies and elves have something to say to you all."

"We are sorry we have caused so much trouble and for casting the spell. We promise to behave from now on and we won't play anymore tricks. We will never cast any spells ever again. We only did it because we felt left out. If we promise to be kinder, could we please join in and all play together?"

Melissa turned to all her friends and asked, "are we in agreement everybody?" "Yes Melissa," they all nodded together. Melissa then turned to the pixies and elves and said, "as you have apologised to us all and promised not to misbehave again of course you can join in with us." With that, everyone danced around with delight.

Chapter 9

Edward had never been so pleased to see Olivia. As the sun's rays danced once again through the branches of the old oak tree, Olivia promised she would include him in everything she did from now on. Edward thanked Olivia for introducing him to her friends. He could see why she loved coming to this magical place but now it was time to go home. They said their goodbyes to their friends and danced and skipped through the woods until they reached the cottage.

They arrived back just in time for supper. Mum asked them if they had had a good day. They both smiled at each other and said together "the best day ever."

The End

About the Author

Barbara Flavell spent her childhood and youth in the rural Welsh county of Pembrokeshire. In her late teens, she swapped the family farm and rugged coastlines for city life in London as she embarked upon a career in nursing, eventually settling in Leicestershire.

She has been married to Tom, a retired solicitor, for over 40 years and has 2 children and 2 grandchildren, who are the inspiration behind her children's stories.

Alongside her love of writing, Barbara is an avid tennis player and keen cook. Barbara writes her children's stories under the pen name Maisy Day, as a nod to memories from her childhood.

Printed in Great Britain
by Amazon